THE ANIMAL BOOGIE

Debbie Harter

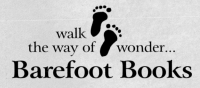

walk
the way of wonder...
Barefoot Books

Down in the jungle, come if you dare!
What can you see shaking here and there?
With a shaky shake here and a shaky shake there,
What's that creature shaking here and there?

IT'S A BEAR!
She goes shake, shake, boogie, woogie, oogie!
Shake, shake, boogie, woogie, oogie!
Shake, shake, boogie, woogie, oogie!
That's the way she's shaking here and there.

Down in the jungle where nobody sees,
What can you see swinging through the trees?
With a swingy swing here and a swingy swing there,
What's that creature swinging through the trees?

IT'S A MONKEY!

He goes swing, swing, boogie, woogie, oogie!

Swing, swing, boogie, woogie, oogie!

Swing, swing, boogie, woogie, oogie!

That's the way he's swinging through the trees.

Down in the jungle in the midday heat,
What can you see stomping its feet?
With a stompy stomp here and a stompy stomp there,
What's that creature stomping its feet?

IT'S AN ELEPHANT!
She goes stomp, stomp, boogie, woogie, oogie!
Stomp, stomp, boogie, woogie, oogie!
Stomp, stomp, boogie, woogie, oogie!
That's the way she's stomping her feet.

Down in the jungle where the trees grow high,
What can you see flying in the sky?
With a flappy flap here and a flappy flap there,
What's that creature flying in the sky?

IT'S A BIRD!
He goes flap, flap, boogie, woogie, oogie!
Flap, flap, boogie, woogie, oogie!
Flap, flap, boogie, woogie, oogie!
That's the way he's flying in the sky.

Down in the jungle where the leaves lie deep,
What can you see learning how to leap?
With a leapy leap here and a leapy leap there,
What's that creature learning how to leap?

IT'S A LEOPARD!
She goes leap, leap, boogie, woogie, oogie!
Leap, leap, boogie, woogie, oogie!
Leap, leap, boogie, woogie, oogie!
That's the way she's learning how to leap.

Down in the jungle where there's danger all around,
What can you see slithering on the ground?
With a slither slither here and a slither slither there,
What's that creature slithering on the ground?

IT'S A SNAKE!

He goes slither, slither, boogie, woogie, oogie!

Slither, slither, boogie, woogie, oogie!

Slither, slither, boogie, woogie, oogie!

That's the way he's slithering on the ground.

Down in the jungle where the stars are shining bright,
Who can you see swaying left and right?
With a sway sway here and a sway sway there,
Who is swaying left and swaying right?

WE ARE!
We go sway, sway, boogie, woogie, oogie!
Sway, sway, boogie, woogie, oogie!
Sway, sway, boogie, woogie, oogie!
That's the way we boogie through the night!

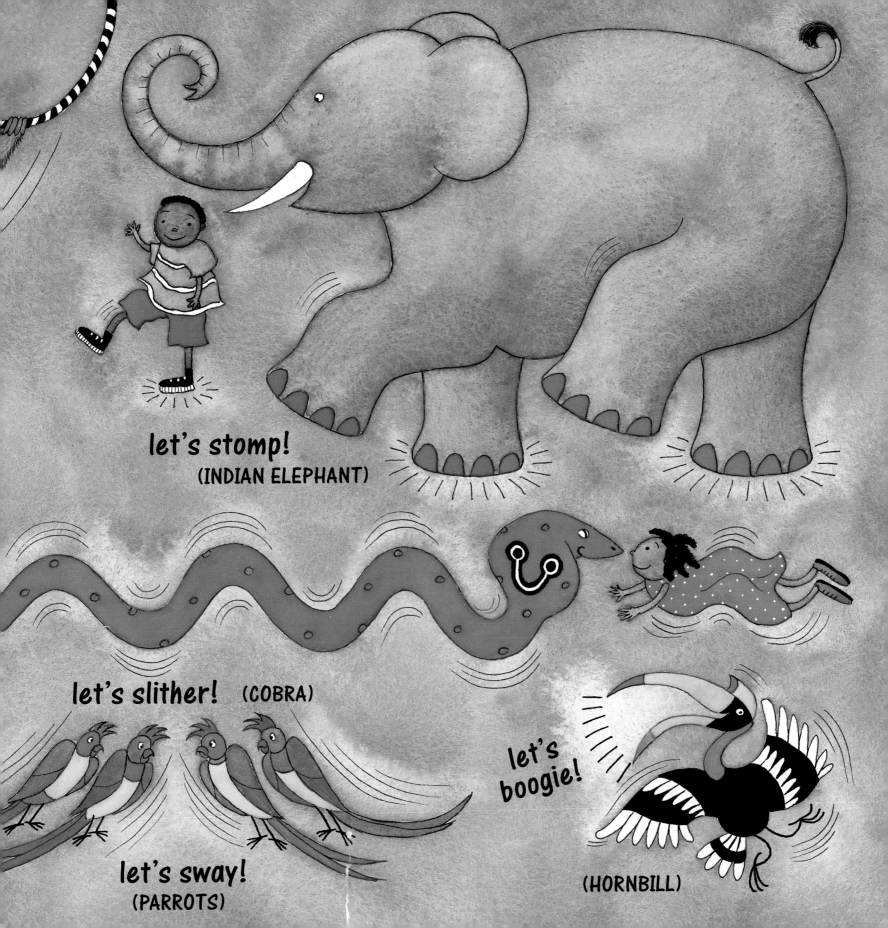

let's stomp!
(INDIAN ELEPHANT)

let's slither! (COBRA)

let's sway!
(PARROTS)

let's boogie!

(HORNBILL)

The Animal Boogie

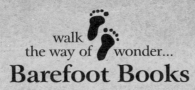

Barefoot Books

The barefoot child symbolizes the human being who is in harmony with the natural world and moves freely across boundaries of many kinds. Barefoot Books explores this image with a range of high-quality picture books for children of all ages. We work with artists, writers and storytellers from many traditions, focusing on themes that encourage independence of spirit, promote understanding and acceptance of different traditions, and foster a life-long love of learning.

www.barefoot-books.com

For Tuppence and Aeron — D. H.
For Suzie and Freya with love — N. T.

Barefoot Books 37 West 17th Street 4th Floor East New York New York 10011
Text copyright © 2000 by Barefoot Books. Illustrations copyright © 2000 by Debbie Harter. The moral right of Debbie Harter to be
identified as the illustrator of this work has been asserted. First published in the United States of America in 2000 by Barefoot Books, Inc. All rights reserved.
No part of this book may be reproduced in any form or by any means, electronic or mechanical, including photocopying, recording or by any information storage and retrieval system, without permission
in writing from the publisher. This book was typeset in One Stroke Script Infant 26 on 30 point. The illustrations were prepared in watercolor, crayon, pen and ink on thick watercolor paper. Graphic design by Judy Linard,
England. Color separation by Grafiscan, Italy. Printed and bound in Singapore by Tien Wah Press (Pte.) Ltd. This book has been printed on 100% acid-free paper.

U.S. Cataloging-in-Publication Data (Library of Congress Standards)
The animal boogie / illustrated by Debbie Harter.-1st ed.
[32]p. : col. ill. ; cm.
Summary: In the jungle, the animals' toes are twitching, their bodies are
wiggling, and their wings are flapping--as they teach children how to do the
Animal Boogie.

ISBN 1-84148-094-0
1. Stories in rhyme. 2. Dance -- Fiction. I. Harter, Debbie, ill. II.
Title.
[E] 21 2000 AC CIP

1 3 5 7 9 8 6 4 2